Creating the Bastard

RYAN NORMAN

Creating the Bastard

Ryan Norman

DEDICATION

To Dr. Johnson, Dr. Hairston, and Mrs. Pharr, my high school principals: Thank you for guiding me through those crucial years and helping me step into adulthood with confidence and purpose.

To my ~~work friends~~ who became my great friends: Lorenzo, Jessica, Sergio, Ronel, Sierran, Tina, Daniel, Jacqueline, Kim, Aaron, Jahvoni, Dana, Angie, Suzann, Katrina, Aaron, Shaniya, Deatherage, Nicholas, John, and Kasey. It was during those challenging days of teaching from home during the COVID-19 pandemic that you all inspired me to chase something greater.

To my best friends, Cedric, Bagwell, Brandon, Harry, C.J., Dre, Dom, Jerome, Aly, Miles, Chris, and Dean: Thank you for your unwavering support and for always encouraging me to keep going.

And to my family—Arlisa, Mom, Antonio, Anna, Jojo, Grandma Carolyn, Isaiah, Logan, David, Aunt Lisa, Aunt Nina, Aunt April, Ebony, Lil Man, Kris, Cam and Dad—thank you for helping me discover and nurture my writing talent. This book would not exist without your love and belief in me.

Table of Contents

Copyright iii

DEDICATION..iv

Chapter 1 8

Chapter 2 16

Chapter 3 29

Chapter 4 35

Chapter 5 40

Chapter 6 49

Chapter 7 56

Chapter 8 61

Chapter 9 67

Chapter 10 72

Chapter 12 82

Chapter 13 87

Chapter 14 94

Chapter 15 101

Chapter 17 112

Chapter 18 119

Chapter 19 124

ABOUT THE AUTHOR 130

Chapter 1

LIGHTS PLEASE
Therapy Session

T.J. SAT IN HIS CAR, glancing at the clock as it neared 3:30 PM.
He wasn't in a hurry to go inside. Instead, he focused on filling out
the intake paperwork, eyes darting between the forms and his
insurance card. His phone, plugged into the auxiliary cord, played
the latest J. Cole album that had dropped on Friday. He checked his
email again, confirming that his insurance covered five free therapy
sessions. The confirmation didn't ease his nerves, but at least he
knew it wouldn't cost him anything—financially, anyway.

As the clock inched closer, T.J. disconnected his phone, took a deep
breath, and stepped out of the car. His steel-toe boots hit the ground
with a dull thud. Dressed in his work hoodie, emblazoned with the
welding company's logo, he headed toward the building—a shared
space with a dentistry and pediatric office, each occupying different
floors.

He walked through the door, handed over the clipboard to the receptionist, and took a seat in the waiting room, his knee bouncing in anticipation.

"Would you like a bottle of water or a soda?" the receptionist asked with a polite smile.

"I'm good, thanks," T.J. replied, wiping his palms on his jeans to dry the nervous sweat that had gathered there. What would his friends think if they knew he was here? What would his family say?

The receptionist looked over the paperwork. "Everything checks out, Travis. Dr. Pharr will see you in room 2, down the hall."

T.J. flinched a little at the use of his full name, but he nodded and stood up. "Thanks," he mumbled as he followed her. The hallway was lined with bright paintings and motivational quotes, none of which made him feel any better.

The receptionist pointed at the door and smiled. "Dr. Pharr will be right with you."

He nodded again, more to himself than to her, and entered the room. It was dimly lit, the soft scent of mango and tangerine hanging in the air from a diffuser in the corner. A small tabletop fountain gurgled quietly, offering a semblance of calm that T.J. didn't feel. He sank into the plush gray sofa, tapping his fingers on his knee, waiting.

After what felt like forever, there was a knock at the door.

"Hello, I'm Dr. Pharr," a warm voice greeted him as she stepped in and extended her hand.

T.J. shook it briefly. "Nice to meet you," he said, trying not to sound as uncomfortable as he felt.

"So, what brings you in today, Travis?" Dr. Pharr asked as she settled into a gray wingback chair across from him.

T.J. shifted, his gaze flicking nervously around the room. "Uh, you can just call me T.J.," he muttered.

"Is that what you prefer?" she asked, pen poised to take notes.

"Yeah. Everyone calls me that. It just feels... weird when people use Travis."

"All right, T.J.," she smiled softly. "So, what's going on?"

T.J. sighed, rubbing his palms together again. "I don't even know where to start. Lately, I've been thinking about the things I've done, and... it doesn't sit right with me."

He paused, trying to find the right words. "I'm with someone right now, and me being here is kinda a condition for her love, I guess. I told her I'd give therapy a shot... for us."

"She must be important to you if you're here for her," Dr. Pharr said, her voice calm and non-judgmental.

"I thought my other baby mothers were important too," T.J. said with a slight smirk. "Guess I just have bad luck."

Dr. Pharr raised an eyebrow. "How many children do you have?"

"Two. My daughter Naomi, she's seven, and my son Joseph, he just turned four. Different moms though." T.J. pulled out his phone, showing her a picture of his kids. "That's them."

"They're beautiful," Dr. Pharr remarked, handing the phone back and jotting down more notes. "How's your relationship with their mothers?"

"It's... fine," T.J. shrugged, leaning back. "I pay my child support and spend time with my kids when I can."

"And when you say your past actions don't sit right with you, are you talking about how things went with the mothers of your children?" Dr. Pharr's eyes met his.

T.J. paused, swallowing. "Yeah, kinda."

"Okay, let's start with Dejah, your first child's mother. How would you describe your relationship with her?"

T.J. laughed bitterly. "Quick. We met at a Halloween party. I was dressed up as 50 Cent—baggy G-Unit clothes and all. She was the Popeyes lady, apron and flour stains on it. Weirdest thing I ever saw, but it worked for her."

"So, you were into her in the beginning?"

"Yeah, I think it was the chase, you know? Once I got her, though... the excitement died, like a firework after it bursts. It all went downhill after that."

Dr. Pharr nodded. "You said she was random and weird. What do you mean by that?"

T.J. ran his hand over his face, shaking his head at the memory. "One day, she drove us to a cemetery out of nowhere. Told me she liked looking at tombstones and imagining what the people's lives were like. I knew then it wasn't going anywhere."

"And how did that make you feel about her?"

"Honestly? Done. I couldn't take her clinginess, especially after we slept together. She told me she loved me, and I couldn't say it back. Then she flipped when she found out I was seeing other women. Got her brother and dad to come after me. I blocked her. Two months later, I got a text from her cousin saying she was pregnant."

"And Raven?"

"We went to the same middle school, but we never talked much. Ran into her at community college—she was studying nursing while I was getting my welding certificate. Seeing a familiar face was nice."

"How would you describe her?"

"Raven's a good girl, really. But I found every excuse not to be with her."

Dr. Pharr paused, looking him over. "Did you love her?"

"No," T.J. replied bluntly.

"Have you ever been in love, T.J.?"

"Yeah," he sighed, waving his hand. "A long time ago."

"How long ago?"

"Freshman year of high school."

Dr. Pharr leaned forward slightly. "Let's start there."

T.J. chuckled, covering his face with his hand. "Man, that story might take up all five sessions."

"That's okay. We've got time," Dr. Pharr said reassuringly.

T.J. exhaled, his shoulders slumping as he leaned back into the couch. "Alright. Freshman year..."

Chapter 2

COLD WORLD

MY EYES FOLLOWED the finger back and forth. Back and forth again. The excruciating sound of the hospital bed paper continued to crinkle as I laid back down on the bed.

"Excuse me, do you have anything for this headache?" I asked, covering my forehead with my forearm.

This was my third time going to the urgent care facility for a head injury in the past two years. I had hoped not to have a concussion. At this point, I do not know what I was more afraid of – my mom finding out that I went to football practice or the doctor coming into the room to inform me that it was another concussion.

As I sat on the bed, I avoided eye contact with my mom who I knew was heated after my last doctor told me not to play anymore contact sports. The fact that she had to leave work to come here due to the athletic trainer having to call her to inform her of my injury made it worse in my head.

Moments passed before the doctor walked into the room. "So, Ms. Gooden, we did determine that Travis has a mild concussion from the collision from the helmets. He will need rest. So, Travis, no physical activities and try to avoid bright lights such as playing video games and watching TV for the first night." The doctor then turned slowly towards my mother. "Mom, he can take some Tylenol for the headaches to manage the pain. Any questions?" The doctor looked as if he knew I was in trouble. He whispered to me as he walked out, "Hang in there, man."

On the way home, I would rather have my mom yell and scream at me. Instead, she called my aunt who was like a grandmother to me to talk to me in her disappointing tone of voice. "Now T.J., you knew better to go out there when your mom and your doctor told you to avoid football after you were getting hit all upside yo' head."

I held the phone to my ear another four times as she called multiple members of my family to embarrass me. This was worse than getting yelled at by her.

My mom, Desiree Gooden, was a nurse. I remember seeing her work very hard in her nursing program to finish. We would visit family members' houses late at night just so she could use a computer to do her work. She loves her job very much and works long hours to pay the bills for me. Unfortunately, at the time, she did not receive enough where she could work a normal 8-hour shift to support the house. So, she worked an enormous number of hours throughout the week which I was grateful for because she could afford to pay the bills and I had the house to myself most of the time.

Five years ago, we moved to Portsmouth in the low-income houses for single parent mothers. It was a nice little 2-bedroom, 1.5-bathroom house. Each house had a little front and backyard. It was nice; however, the area was drug and crime infested. Every day, I would either hear gunshots, someone fighting outside, or police sirens in the neighborhood.

When we first moved to the neighborhood, I was lucky to meet my two best friends: Dedric and Bryson. Since fourth grade, we were always in the same classes. The three of us really bonded through playing football. It was our thing. We would watch football from

Wednesday through Monday together during the football season; Wednesday was the middle school games, Thursdays was JV Football, Fridays was the local Varsity games, Saturday was College Football on TV, Sunday was for NFL games, and Monday was the ESPN football game.

We played middle school football from 7th to 8th grade. We were so good. Dedric played Defensive End because of his wide, tall frame and quick speed off the line to get many sacks on the quarterback. I played Outside Linebacker. Even though I was very small, I had the heart to tackle anyone in my proximity – no matter how big they were. Bryson was the fastest of us all. He played cornerback and managed to lock up every wide receiver that he checked.

When Coach Taylor came to watch all our games, we knew that we would be skipping JV to play Varsity our freshman year. We would talk all night about what college we all were going to play for.

Around this time, we were known around the hood as the *"Cool little dudes that played football"*. This helped us so much as it made some of the OG's in the hood keep us out of harm's way.

As my mother cooked me a quick pot of spaghetti to eat before she went back to work, she remained on the phone with her sisters as they would frequently do conference calls to keep in touch with each other. I was hoping that she would somehow, magically forget what I did. As she was leaving the house to finish her shift at work, she yelled, "And I'm going to call the school tomorrow morning and make sure you don't play!".

That crushed me. I texted my girl, Natalie what happened. I also wrote in the group chat to tell Dedric and Bryson to meet me outside on my porch in 10 minutes. They both stayed within two minutes from me.

When I got outside with my chair to put on the porch, I seen my boys walking from both directions with chairs over their heads. It was a rule from the rental office that we could not have porch chairs due to the heavy loitering in the neighborhood. One night, when we sat on the ground, Bryson had a roach crawl under his shirt. Since then, we refused to sit on the ground. So, we just keep our chair near the front door in our houses.

"Yo, the doctors told me that I can't play anymore. I got too many concussions." I told them as we sat on the porch with the moonlight and streetlights beaming in my eyes.

"Damn, bro! You talk to Coach Taylor yet?" Dedric asked as he looked up concussion symptoms on his phone privately.

"Yeah man, you need to call him to let him know?" Bryson replied.

"For what? I do not feel like hearing his mouth right now. It's kinda' his fault anyway to keep telling me that he needed me out there." I exclaimed to them suddenly.

As I was talked to Dedric, Bryson hands me his phone, "He right here coach." Bryson cackled as he watch me grab the phone from his hands.

"Yeah, Coach?" I murmured. For some strange reason, I could instantly tell that he was very worried over the phone.

"You good, T.J.? Was it a concussion? Coach Taylor asked anxiously.

"Yeah coach, my mom told me I can't play anymore since this my third concussion." I remarked.

Coach Taylor made a noise of confusion. "What you mean this is your third concussion boy?"

"Yeah, I had two concussions last year. I thought Coach Thomas told you." I replied.

Coach Taylor took a deep sigh. "Man, that dude ain't tell me nothing like that. I'll call him tomorrow. I would have never rushed you out there like that T.J. Believe me on that! That's my word!" Coach Taylor continued to talk. "So, what are you gonna do?"

I took a second to think. "Um, I don't know. I'll probably go help out at the concession stand or something to sell hotdogs and weed." I suggested getting a laugh from Dedric and Bryson. I did not hear Coach Taylor laughing, at all.

"That's not funny man. Listen, I have a proposition for you. I need you to hear me out before you decline." Coach Taylor took a while before he could gather his thoughts. "I know you wanna' be out there wit yo' boys. How about you come out there to be the team manager and I'll teach you a thing or two about football."

Dedric and Bryson started to laugh as I became a little embarrassed. "Coach Taylor, I am not about to be out there being a damn water boy. What I look like?"

"Now did I ask you to be a water boy and watch your damn mouth!" Coach Taylor shouted.

"My fault coach. And no, you didn't ask me to serve water." I paused for a brief moment. "So, what will I be out there doing?" I mumbled.

"Washing the jerseys and preparing them for game day and helping me and the coaches plan for the game. Um, look, you will still be a part of the football team. You just won't be playing. I'll give you a jersey and everything." Coach Taylor implied. "So, what's up? Do you want to do it or not?"

I looked at Dedric and Bryson as they both mouthed the word yes to me. "I guess so." I paused for a moment and took a deep breath as tears began to race down my face from both eyes. "Yeah, I'll do it coach!".

Chapter 3

SIDELINE STORY

WALKING INTO THE LOCKER ROOM for the first time was nerve-wracking. My heart raced, the same way it always did before the first play of a game, or whenever I had to talk to random girls, or walk into an unfamiliar place. Coach Taylor had told me to show up for the film session to ease into things, but even after the session, I felt like a stranger in a place that used to feel like home.

After the film, Coach Taylor stood up in front of the team. "One more thing before we head out to the field," he said, and then his eyes found me, sitting at the back of the room. "Unfortunately, T.J. won't be playing this year due to a head injury. It's a loss for the team—big hopes for him on defense this year. But he's staying with us as the team manager, and I need you to show him the same respect as you'd give to anyone on the coaching staff."

I shifted in my seat as whispers filled the room. The embarrassment was instant, like a weight on my chest. Coach's plan to build rapport by keeping the team in the locker room for thirty minutes before heading to practice wasn't helping. I could feel eyes on me, players murmuring as I walked around with a notebook, jotting down their numbers to make sure I got their practice jerseys ready for the next day.

"You good, T.J.? I heard you got CTE or something from that hit you tried to put on me," Rocket said with a grin, loud enough for everyone to hear. Laughter erupted. Damon "Rocket" Knight was the quarterback—decent player, with some college offers, but a big talker.

I wanted to get mad, but I knew better. Instead, I played along, masking the frustration.

"I don't know, man. Probably," I shot back, keeping my tone light. "Maybe from hitting my head on Tia's headboard a few too many times."

The room burst into laughter, and I caught Rocket's eyes shift. He smiled, but it was nervous. I had done my homework before the season started, looking up all the star players on social media. I knew Rocket liked to clown on people, and I came prepared. Found plenty of pictures of him and his girl, Tia, and some other stuff on his mom's Facebook. If I had to, I had ammo ready. But I held back.

"Nah, you got CTE from getting your ass trucked!" Rocket fired back, his voice tense.

I raised my hands in mock surrender. "You got it, man!" I said, laughing as I continued jotting down jersey numbers. No need to burn through my jokes in one session, and I wasn't about to disrespect one of the senior leaders. I wanted respect too, even if I wasn't on the field.

Jermaine, who had been watching from the side, jumped in. "I don't know if he got trucked, Rocket. He put a big hit on you!" Jermaine laughed, giving my shoulder a light squeeze. "You gotta remember, you weren't wearing your red jersey, so you were asking for it, man!"

A red jersey during practice meant no contact. Rocket didn't have one on that day, so I knew I could lay him out. I had to. I wanted my teammates to see I wasn't afraid, even though Rocket was a good six-three, two-fifteen.

"Yeah, whatever, man!" Rocket said, changing the subject, trying to take a shot at me. "You talking about girls now, huh? Ain't no telling what your white girl is doing over at Peninsula."

The locker room erupted again with a collective "Daaaamn!" as Rocket brought up Natalie, my girlfriend. I hadn't expected that, and the fact that he knew about her caught me off guard.

But again, I just raised my hands, laughing it off. "You got it, man!"

Dedric, trying to shift the mood, asked, "Speaking of girls, who are the freaks at this school?"

Laughter and wild stories filled the air, and I let out a breath. It was wild, listening to all these stories. They felt like lies—maybe they weren't, but it didn't matter. I just sat back and absorbed the chaos.

Then, from the corner of the room, someone yelled, "Yo, Jermaine! You don't gotta worry about all this freak talk. Sade's got a damn chastity belt on!"

I tensed, waiting for Jermaine to blow up, but he just laughed and tossed a towel at the guy. Cool, laidback, unbothered. I admired that. I wasn't sure I could stay that calm if someone clowned on my girl like that.

Jermaine and Sade had been together forever, since I moved to Portsmouth. Sade lived next door to me, and her mom, Ms. Anderson, used to watch me in the mornings when my mom left for work early. I even remember the day Jermaine told Sade he liked her, stealing the bus driver's mic to announce it to everyone. Since then, they'd been inseparable.

Later, sitting next to Dedric and Bryson, I couldn't shake what Rocket said. "How do you think he knows about Natalie?" Bryson asked.

"I don't know. Maybe he saw us together somewhere," I shrugged.

Practice started, and as the team hit the field, I set up the camera to record. Coach Taylor had told me to film the session and wash the jerseys afterward. While the camera rolled, I pulled out my phone and texted Natalie, asking if she knew anyone named Rocket. She just laughed and said no.

After practice, I washed the gear, folded the jerseys, and stacked them for the next day. On the drive home, Coach Taylor couldn't stop talking about the team. He believed this was the year we'd make the playoffs. "This team is special," he said, looking at Dedric and Bryson in the rearview. "I brought you young guys up because I know you've got what it takes. Your chemistry, your hard work—it'll rub off on the rest of them."

Dedric and Bryson lit up, and I smiled for them. But inside, I felt hollow. They were going to keep playing, keep shining, and I... I was on the sidelines.

Chapter 4

SESSION TWO
Therapy Session

DR. PHARR LEANED BACK IN HER CHAIR, her eyes scanning over her notes from their last session. She took a deep breath before speaking. "You seemed pretty nervous coming in last time. How are you feeling today, T.J.?"

T.J. rubbed his hands across his work pants, his eyes drifting toward the ceiling. "I feel more comfortable today. It's not as bad as I thought it would be."

Dr. Pharr smiled, a glint of encouragement in her eyes. "That's progress! You should be proud. It's not easy for most people to open up to someone new."

T.J. nodded, taking a deep breath. "You're right. Thanks."

"So, last time we left off with the ride home after your practice with Coach Taylor. We'll get back to that, but first…" Dr. Pharr leaned forward, crossing her legs and meeting his gaze. "Let's dig a little deeper."

T.J. shifted, caught off guard. "How deep?"

"Don't worry," Dr. Pharr said, leaning back again, her pen tapping lightly on her notepad. "Let's start with something basic. Growing up, how would you describe your relationship with your parents?"

T.J.'s eyebrows raised, confusion settling on his face. "What does my relationship with my parents have to do with anything I'm here for now?"

"That's a fair question," Dr. Pharr acknowledged, scribbling a quick note. "Our parents are often our first and most significant relationship. Their dynamics set the foundation for how we interact in future relationships."

"And?" T.J. straightened in his chair, waiting for more.

"Well, we tend to carry certain patterns from those early relationships into our romantic lives as adults It's not always obvious, but have you ever noticed certain behaviors you might have picked up from your parents?" Dr. Pharr's tone was calm but probing.

T.J. hesitated. "I don't know… I don't think that's true. I'm my own man. I'd never be like my dad."

Dr. Pharr nodded thoughtfully. "That's a common feeling. But the way love is shown—or isn't shown—during childhood often influences how we express love later on. For example, love can be conveyed through affection, words of encouragement, gifts, or it can be absent altogether."

T.J. considered her words for a moment before speaking. "So, you're saying whatever I saw as a kid is how I'm gonna treat people now?"

"Not exactly," Dr. Pharr clarified. "But those early examples— whether positive or negative—can shape how we communicate love or handle conflict. For instance, if love was conditional or inconsistent, you might find it hard to trust or express yourself fully in adult relationships."

T.J. leaned forward slightly, interested now. "What else do we take from our parents into our relationships?"

"In addition to how we show love, how we manage anger or tension is another big factor. Many of us unconsciously model the way our parents handled conflict, whether it's through silence, passive aggression, or outright verbal aggression."

T.J. chuckled, a little uneasily. "You know, I've been told I act 'female-ish' when I'm mad."

Dr. Pharr raised an eyebrow. "Who told you that? And why do you think they said it?"

"These two girls I used to date," T.J. admitted. "I guess it's because when I'm mad, I don't talk. I shut down, isolate myself. I avoid the fight instead of facing it."

Dr. Pharr frowned slightly. "It's unfortunate they described it that way. There's no right or wrong way to express your emotions. Everyone handles conflict differently, and how you choose to react is your own."

T.J. shrugged. "Yeah, I get that."

"Here's the thing," Dr. Pharr continued. "How we manage—or avoid—anger often mirrors how we saw it handled in our family growing up. For example, in my family, conflict was addressed openly. But in other families, like my husband's, it was often met with silence or passive-aggressive behavior. Some families use harsh words that can leave emotional scars. All of these methods shape how we engage in conflict as adults."

T.J. leaned back, the weight of her words sinking in. There was a pause as Dr. Pharr let the moment settle.

Finally, she broke the silence. "Shall we pick up where we left off, with your freshman year?"

Chapter 5

WET DREAMS

MY FEELINGS FOR WEEKENDS varied on which weekend it was. On the first and last weekend of each month, I would work with my cousin, Peanut, and my Uncle Mel. My Uncle Mel had a construction business and would look out for me by allowing me to help him out on the worksites to earn money for school clothes and other things if I needed to help my mom out. Peanut was three years older than me and was like an older brother to me.

My uncle paid me a whopping $10 an hour which was so much money for 14-year-old. Even though the money was good, the work was so hard. It started with me working every day in the summertime. I just wanted to do the weekends to give my young body a rest.

One day, I would be assigned to dig to create a foundation so they could come behind me to begin to lay bricks or I would be asked to make multiple batches of mortar in a wheelbarrow and a shovel.

It was fun most of the time too. My Uncle Mel would allow me to measure and cut cinder blocks with chainsaws and pass them to the masons. I even got to help on a project to build a new auditorium for my elementary school that I went to. It was cool to visit places and think to myself, "I helped build that!". It felt good to have extra money in my pockets at times to look out for my boys when we went places.

On the weekends that I didn't work with my cousin and uncle, I helped volunteer at the Rec Center. In the neighborhood, the city repeatedly removed the hoops from the basketball courts outside due to multiple kids getting shot from stray bullets that weren't even meant for them. I never wanted to be in a place where me or my friends could possibly get shot.

Me and my friends loved to play basketball in our spare time. When we were not inside playing the game, we were at the courts challenging anyone from grown men in their primes to little kids in 3 on 3 basketball games. For some reason, Dedric had this amazing jump shot that would be an almost guaranteed bucket when he shot it. Bryce was very quick and could blow by anyone guarding him.

Myself on the other hand, I was okay. I could play defense and make good passes. I would sometimes miss everything that I shot and sometime, I would become hot and make everything I shot.

To get runs in on the basketball court, I begged the local Rec Center director, Mrs. Hairston to allow me to volunteer. My mom could not afford to pay for a membership so for 2 days straight, I took the city bus to the Rec Center. I brought along my book bag with glass cleaner, rags, and bleach sanitizer. I picked up trash in the parking lots, emptied the outside trash cans, cleaned the windows, and sanitized the doors until she finally saw me on camera.

Mrs. Hairston admired my dedication so much, she allowed me to volunteer with the school age kids for summer camp, after school camp and the weekends. She also would allow me to bring Dedric and Bryson during open gym hours to play basketball as long as we had our parent signatures or consent each time.

I met my girlfriend, Natalie, on a teen dating website last year and she was very cool. We liked all of the same music, same movies and shows, shoes and she played Volleyball which made me even more attracted to her due her competitive spirit. The only minor issue with us was that I was black, and she was white. I didn't care though because I didn't raise myself to see color, only the individual. Even though we stayed in the same city, there were not more than 2 white families in my neighborhood.

When Natalie would come pick me up, it was cool for her to take me places that I haven't been to. One night, she called and told me to get dressed and that she was going to pick me up and go on a date.

Being the gentleman that I was, I would pay for the dates with the money that I earned from working with my uncle and she would do the driving since she had her license.

"Let's just go watch a movie and then we can find something to eat after." Natalie implied.

I shrugged my shoulders. "That's cool with me. What movies are out?"

"Let's just pick when we get there." Natalie said while driving. Natalie and I liked the same music so she would burn our favorite songs onto a CD to pop in the CD player when we were on the way to places.

Around this time, the power of hormones began to overtake my body. That was mixed with the explicit sexual stories I would hear from the guys in the locker room. I felt like I was ready to explode. I was ready to do anything to be in the position of not being a virgin anymore. Natalie lost her virginity to her last boyfriend before me.

Before we became official boyfriend and girlfriend, she would tell me that she loved the feeling of sex and could not wait to find someone to do it with. At the time, it was not something that I was hyped up for because Natalie said that she wanted to get to know me more before we did it. I was focused on football and having fun with my friends. Now that football was out of the picture, I had to focus on one thing – losing my virginity. Just as I would do for football, I studied film to make sure when it was time for it to happen, I would be ready.

Pulling up to the movie theater, there was only one movie that was available at the time. It was some R-rated romantic drama. The guy that worked at the ticket booth didn't even care that we were underage. He gave us the tickets and told us to "Hurry up!" in the movie. We walked very fast while laughing into the theater. The first scene of the movie was a sex scene. Furthermore, throughout the movie, it was sex scene after sex scene. It became very cringey; it was like we were watching soft porn. It made me feel super uncomfortable for some reason. The level of discomfort was on the same scale of watching a sex or kissing scene with my mom. I instantly became stressed, but sexually aroused at the same time due to me being stressed out. This was due to the look of Natalie's eyes during the sex scenes. It felt as if she was mentally connected to them while I am being supremely skirmish in my seat.

After the movie, to break the ice while in the car I looked at Natalie, "It was like we were watching a damn flick in the theater." I commented while laughing.

"Right! I don't know why there were so many sex scenes!" Natalie asserted while laughing also. "So instead of going to a restaurant, you wanna' just stop at McDonald's or something then I can take you home?"

"Damn, you read my mind! I'm tired as hell after that boring movie." I acknowledged.

Natalie rubbed her fingers through my hair. "I'm sorry T.J."

On the way to my house, I was amped. I was ready to ask Natalie for sex, however, I didn't know how to ask without coming off aggressive.

"Yo, pull over so we can have sex." I thought to myself. *"Nah! That's not going to work. Yo Natalie, you think you ready to have sex with ya' boy?"* Immediately, I realized my mind was going crazier than ever before.

After five minutes of hesitatingly thinking to myself, I finally built up enough confidence to ask.

I turned down the radio so she could hear me speak. "Hey, um, when do you think we could do what they were doing in the movie?"

Natalie., without delay, reached in her arm rest and slid a ticket on my lap.

A roar of laughter escaped my mouth and then exclaimed, "What is this? A pass to have sex with you or something?

Natalie rolled her eyes. "Ha ha. No fool! It's a ticket for my fall prom.

My laughter switched to skepticism. "But you're in the 10th grade. I thought prom was only for 11th and 12th graders.

"At my school, they give the freshman and sophomores their own prom in the fall and the upperclassman's prom is in the spring near graduation time." Natalie replied.

"That's dope!" I said with a perplexed tone.

Natalie looked at me and stated, "I need you to think about why I gave you the ticket when you asked that."

I paused for a moment and finally said, "To change the conversation."

"That ticket date answers your question silly. We can have sex the night of prom." Natalie affirmed.

As much as I wanted to scream and shout, I remained as calm and smooth as a Kenny G song. "That's cool." I replied.

"I need you to get a tux. I was thinking of wearing our favorite colors – blue and black. What do you think?" Natalie suggested.

"I'm with it." I picked up the ticket from my lap and read the details. *Doors open at 6 p.m. on November 14.* "Natalie, is this prom in 6 weeks like I just read on this ticket?"

Natalie smirked. "Well, it is the Fall."

"Why are you just now telling me about this?" I contented.

"I just brought the tickets today. I didn't want to go but my friends begged me to come and to bring you along with me. You mad at me?"

I looked at the ticket and looked at Natalie. "Nah, I'm not mad. I'm actually happy to go in there dancing to Justin Timberlake with the white folks." I laughed out loud.

"Ha ha! You been having a lot of jokes tonight. I'll call you when I get home." Natalie then reached over to kiss me before I got out of the car to go in the house.

Chapter 6

CHERISH THE DAY

A RAPID BUZZ AGAINST my nightstand startled me awake. My phone was blowing up with text messages.

"Yo, come outside to your porch," Bryce's message read.

Still groggy, I dragged myself out of bed, splashed some water on my face, and grabbed the porch chair. When I stepped outside, Bryce and Dedric were deep into a game of curb ball.

Now, curb ball is the ultimate hood game, a street classic. We picked it up after the city took down the basketball rims. The rules are simple: you throw a basketball at the curb, aiming to hit the top edge just right to make the ball fly. Hit it, and you get another shot, racking up points. First to ten wins.

Dedric and Bryce were taking it seriously. Dedric talks so much trash it makes you want to spear him like Brock Lesnar. Bryce, on the other hand, keeps it low-key until he decides to talk, and when he does, it's like a slap in the face. I usually stay out of their beef because they always think I'm picking sides when I'm just trying to keep the peace.

A new text buzzed on my phone. It was from Natalie.

"Hey! How's the tux situation going?" she asked.

"I'll get fitted sometime this week," I texted back, trying to sound casual.

Prom was around the corner, and the anticipation of finally losing my virginity was giving me tunnel vision. Before I could dwell on that, another text popped up from Natalie.

"Sounds like a plan! I'll call you when I'm off work."

I quickly refocused. "Yo! I got next!" I shouted to Bryce and Dedric, desperate to get my mind off prom night.

"10! Game over, bum!" Dedric yelled, dancing around like he won the NBA Finals.

"Nah, run it back!" Bryce snapped, not ready to accept defeat.

Dedric, still hyped, waved me over. "Nah! Next!" he hollered.

Bryce, holding up a hand, said, "Hold up, T.J.! I'm about to whoop him again."

I waved them off, laughing, and glanced at my phone, checking for NFL updates.

Suddenly, Mary J. Blige's voice drifted through the air. Ms. Anderson pulled into her driveway in that old station wagon with the fake wood panels—the kind you only see in retro movies. Her car was packed like she was hosting a family reunion, groceries overflowing from the trunk and back seat.

Back and forth, she went, hauling bags into the house. I glanced at Dedric and Bryce, still locked in their curb ball battle, then made up my mind.

"I got you, Ms. Anderson," I said, jogging over to help.

"Thank you, baby!" she said, a bead of sweat forming on her forehead.

We tag-teamed the bags, bringing in what felt like a week's worth of snacks—chips, cupcakes, ice cream, popsicles, and an endless supply of cookies. At the bottom of the pile was a huge box, big enough to hold a dresser.

"Grab this end, T.J.," she instructed.

"This thing's massive! You building a shoe closet or something?" I joked, struggling to get a grip.

Ms. Anderson laughed. "It's a desk for Sade. She needs somewhere better to do her homework than her bed."

I chuckled, pointing to the table. "Well, she better use it then."

"She will, eventually," Ms. Anderson said with a smile.

As we finished, she wiped her hands and glanced at me. "You can unpack everything. Just put it near me, and I'll organize. You can toss the bags in that cabinet."

Just as I was finishing up, I heard the back door creak open. Sliding footsteps shuffled closer until Sade appeared, wearing one of Jermaine's football shorts and a black tank top.

We weren't as close as we used to be. The air between us was always weird now—awkward.

"Hey, T.J.," Sade greeted, her voice soft.

I nodded back.

"Ma, why didn't you call me to help?" she asked, looking a bit guilty.

"I didn't want to bother you while you were working," Ms. Anderson replied. "Besides, T.J. saw an old lady struggling and stepped up." She laughed.

Sade brought her laptop to the kitchen, asking her mom to check over a PowerPoint presentation.

Trying to ease the tension, I asked, "Is that for that tough English teacher everyone complains about?"

"Nah, it's for my Early Childhood class," Sade explained, her voice lighter. "I have to come up with ten activities for the kids. And I have to demo three of them with my classmates. It's a nightmare."

"You got this, girl!" Ms. Anderson chimed in.

"I don't know," Sade sighed. "It's due Tuesday, and it's like 30 percent of my grade."

Ms. Anderson turned to me after the last grocery bag was emptied. "T.J., you and your boys wanna build this desk? I'll order some pizza."

"Ma, Jermaine and I could've done that," Sade protested.

Ms. Anderson playfully glanced around. "And where is Jermaine now?"

My stomach growled, and I played it cool. "Yeah, we can do it. I'll ask them, but I'm sure they're free."

I was about to grab Dedric and Bryce when it hit me—I had volunteering at the Rec Center tomorrow.

I turned back to Sade. "You know, I could help you with your project. I volunteer with kids at the Rec, and we do activities all the time."

Sade raised an eyebrow. "You think you can help me with this? Curb ball and football aren't exactly what I'm looking for."

I laughed. "Nah, I've got better stuff. You could even come with me to the Rec tomorrow. It might give you some ideas."

Sade hesitated. "Will they let me come?"

"They should. Let me check." I dashed outside to call the Rec Center.

After a few minutes on hold, Mrs. Hairston picked up. "Hey, T.J.! What's up?"

"Hey! I've got a friend who needs help with a project for her Early Childhood class. Can she volunteer tomorrow?"

"Of course! Just have her fill out the paperwork when she comes in."

I walked back into the house, trying to play it cool.

"So, can I come?" Sade asked.

"Yep. Be ready by 9 a.m. We'll catch the bus."

Sade and Ms. Anderson laughed. "We'll take my mom's car," Sade affirmed.

Chapter 7

CHAINING DAY

GETTING A CHANCE to hang out with Sade again was mind-boggling—in a good way. It felt like a door had cracked open, a chance to get us back on speaking terms—at the very least. Maybe, just maybe, she could help me figure out how to become class president like she was. I needed to branch out now that football wasn't my only focus.

After we finished putting together Sade's desk and stuffed ourselves with pizza, it hit me—I promised my uncle I'd help him and my cousin with some work this weekend. I started pacing in my room, trying to think of an excuse that wouldn't get me chewed out. Finally, I had it.

I grabbed my phone and scrolled down to Uncle Mel's number. "Hey, Unc!"

"What's up, T.J.?" His voice came through, deep and steady.

"I've had this killer headache all weekend. I was waiting to see if it'd go away before calling, but I'm still feeling dizzy," I lied, layering on the misery for effect.

"Oh damn! That's rough. Those concussions are no joke." He sounded concerned. "Don't worry, we're just digging a foundation for an add-on. Me and Peanut can handle it."

A grin spread across my face before I replied. "I appreciate it, Uncle Mel. I'm really sorry, man."

"Rest up and stay hydrated, Nephew!" He hung up, and before the call even ended, I was already jumping around my room like a kid with extra recess time. One more day to hang with Sade? I'd take it.

After playing video games all night and eating everything in sight, I crashed for a couple of hours. My alarm went off at 9:00 AM, and I shot out of bed, ready. I grabbed my rec center volunteer shirt, showered, and dressed. I glanced at the clock—9:25 AM. Plenty of time. From my closet, I pulled out my good Jordans, the ones I saved for special occasions like dances and dates.

When I stepped outside, Sade was already there, leaning against her car. The sunlight bounced off her, making her look even more relaxed. She looked at my shoes and grinned. "I've been waiting on you, Mr. Fresh."

I smiled awkwardly, caught off guard. "I said we could leave at 10," I replied, embarrassed.

We got in the car, buckled up, and hit the road toward the rec center. The silence hung heavy for the first minute or so until Sade broke it. "You ain't never heard a sound system like this."

I gave her a sideways glance. "What do you mean by that?"

She smirked and reached up to the sun visor, pulling out a CD. "This is what I mean." She slid it into the stereo, and the car erupted with sound—BOOM! BOOM! BOOM! I looked at the mirrors and windows, vibrating like we were front row at a concert.

"I remember how you always wanted those bass-boosted headphones," she said, her voice cutting through the music as she turned the volume down a bit.

"It's all about the bass," I grinned, feeling a wave of nostalgia.

Sade smiled back before turning the music up again. As the beats thumped, I couldn't help but think how surprising it was that she remembered that little detail about me. And to top it off, she was playing my favorite song. The moment couldn't have been better.

"Hey, can we stop there?" I yelled over the music, pointing to a McDonald's.

Sade laughed, "I'm broke at the moment."

"I got you!" I said, my stomach growling. We pulled into the drive-thru, and Sade squinted at the menu, searching for the dollar options.

"What are you getting?" she asked.

"I might grab the chicken biscuit combo—with strawberry jelly," I said, scanning the choices. I glanced over at her still peering at the small print. "Get whatever you want. It's on me."

She seemed caught off guard, like no one had ever made that offer before. She ordered the same combo, and we ate in the parking lot, the sound of the bass still echoing in the background. Between bites, she mentioned that her mom's ex-boyfriend had installed the system

in the car before going to jail for selling drugs. I nodded, trying to

piece together the parts of her life I had missed.

Chapter 8

CHAINING DAY PART II

WALKING INTO THE REC CENTER, I felt like I was on top of the world, though I couldn't quite place why. At first, I thought it was the fit—catching my reflection in the glass as we walked in— but it had to be more than that. The rec was always packed with college kids from the HBCU up the street who worked there. Most of them were cool, always looking out for me, though they liked to tease me like I was their little brother. The vibe there was fun, laid-back.

As we stepped inside, I noticed some of the guys and girls glancing my way, smiling when they saw Sade with me. That's when I knew—it wasn't the fit. It was her. She had me feeling like the big man on campus without even trying.

Sade, back then, was about 5'3" or 5'4". Skin like Alicia Keys, and a face that reminded you of a young Raven-Symoné. She had that blend of curvy and fit that made heads turn. The kind of pretty, nerdy hood girl you'd find in most neighborhoods.

"Hey, Mrs. Hairston! This is Sade," I said as we stood at the door of her office.

"Hey! Nice to meet you, Sade," Mrs. Hairston greeted her warmly. "Once you fill out the paperwork, T.J. can show you around and introduce you to everyone."

While Sade filled out her paperwork, Mrs. Hairston pulled me aside with a grin. "I see you, T.J.! Using the kids to reel in a new girlfriend?"

I laughed. "Nah, Mrs. Hairston, I'm just here to help."

When Sade finished, she said, "I think I'm done, Mrs. Hairston."

"Great! If you have any more questions, just come back here. I'm here to help," Mrs. Hairston said as we made our way toward the break room.

"She's so nice," Sade remarked.

"She really is," I agreed.

I wanted to introduce Sade to the crew before we got to the activities with the kids. "Hey y'all, this is Sade. She'll be volunteering today," I announced as we entered the break room.

While Sade chatted with some of the college girls about why she came, a few of the guys gave me fist pounds—silent acknowledgment that Sade was definitely a catch.

I caught Sade before the girls talked her ear off, and we headed to the gym. The second we opened the door, a group of kids came running up to me.

"T.J.! You're here!" they shouted, swarming me.

"Hey, everyone! This is Sade. She's helping us out today—she's really cool," I said, introducing her to the kids, who were all buzzing with energy.

"Is she your girlfriend, T.J.?" one little girl asked, sending a ripple of giggles through the group.

"Nah, she's been my friend for a while. She's in 11th grade at my school, and she's also the class president," I told them.

"What's a class president?" one kid asked.

"Well, she does cool stuff like planning parties, field trips, and even helps people when they need it. Like this one time, a kid's house burned down, and she started a fundraiser to help his family."

"So, she's like Obama but for school?" another kid chimed in.

"Basically. Alright, enough questions—let's have some fun!"

I ran over to the nearest station, but not before glancing back at Sade, who looked impressed.

"How did you know all that? We haven't talked in forever," Sade whispered as she caught up to me.

"I keep up with my friends," I replied with a grin.

Time flew by as the kids pulled Sade to different stations— basketball, making slime, planting beans, ice cube painting, and even building Alka-Seltzer rockets.

I spent most of the time at the slime station with Davion, a kid with autism. He was high-functioning but didn't do well socially. When

Sade came over to introduce herself, Davion ran behind me, refusing to talk.

Sade laughed and joked, "Is that your son?"

I pulled her aside. "Davion has autism. He doesn't really talk to people he doesn't know."

"Oh my God, I didn't know! I'm so sorry," Sade exclaimed, her face flushing with embarrassment.

"It's cool," I reassured her as we headed back to the station.

Back at the slime station, I knelt beside Davion. "Hey, buddy, this is my friend Sade. Guess what? Her favorite show is *Autobots*."

Sade gave me a confused look, and I mouthed, "Just go with it."

Davion's eyes lit up. "Who's your favorite bot?"

I slid my phone to Sade, pulling up a page about *Autobots* to give her some context.

"I like Sally because she's pink and nice," Sade said, rolling with the improvisation. Davion's face lit up as he grabbed Sade's hand, his fingers covered in slime and led her to the next station. She shot me a grateful look, mouthing, "Thank you."

In that moment, I couldn't help but wonder—could Natalie ever come here and make the same impact with the kids the way Sade just did?

Chapter 9

NO ORDINARY LOVE

LEADING UP TO THE PROM, I made sure everything was checked off my list. The tux—fitted black with a midnight blue vest peeking under the jacket—was tailored just right. I got my haircut sharp with the bigen lined up perfectly on the edges and picked up the corsage. I'd even saved enough money for after the dance, planning to impress Natalie later. Originally, my cousin Peanut was supposed to drop me off at Natalie's, but his car broke down at the last minute. That left me with my usual ride—the city bus.

As I left the house, my mom texted, "Have fun at the dance!" I didn't have the energy to tell her it was really prom. If she'd known, there was no way she would've let me step foot on the bus in a tux.

"I'll try!" I replied, keeping it short. No need for extra attention.

Walking onto the bus, I felt like the man. The tuxedo had me looking sharp—fitted jacket over a crisp white shirt, bow tie tight. I texted Natalie, "I'm on the way. Be there in 30 minutes!"

The bus ride was like a strange dream. People were extra nice, from single moms wrangling their kids to the businessmen on their evening commute. Even the driver waved off the fare. I guess a tuxedo makes everyone act right. I felt untouchable.

When I got off at the stop closest to Natalie's house, my ego was boosted beyond measure. People on the bus called out, wishing me luck, like I was walking into a movie scene. But as I started the ten-minute walk to her place, that high started to fade. My stomach tightened with familiar anxiety. Was it the thought of being around her white classmates? Or the reality that tonight, I might lose my virginity?

Right before reaching her house, I caught a glimpse of myself in the reflection of her car. It was parked by a big bush that partially hid the house. I checked my hairline for any of the bigen running down from the barbershop. A deep breath steadied me as I took a few steps closer. Then I saw it.

Confederate flags. Everywhere.

The mailbox was painted in red, white, and blue. A flagpole with the same flag waved proudly by the side of the house. Her dad's truck, parked in the driveway, had a massive sticker that said, "YES, I am a REDNECK!" A sick feeling crawled over me. This wasn't the warm welcome I had hoped for.

I texted Natalie, "Hey, I'm outside."

"Just ring the doorbell, silly," she replied.

I hesitated. My pulse pounded in my ears as I imagined what was waiting behind that door. Taking a deep breath, I rang the bell.

The top latch clicked. My heart sank when I saw who answered. Natalie's dad stood there—big, burly, and disheveled in a white T-shirt and boxers. His face wore an expression of annoyance like I was interrupting his evening. "Hey, my name is T.J. Nice to meet you," I said, my voice steadier than I felt.

He didn't acknowledge my words, just waved me in. "Wait here," he said before hollering upstairs, "Natalie! Your friend's here!"

I stood awkwardly in the hallway, glancing around. The place was decked out with deer heads and family photos—everything screamed small-town, country living. Her mom peeked around the corner, waved, then disappeared. I was expecting at least a quick conversation, something friendly. But no.

Finally, Natalie came down the stairs. She looked stunning. My nerves quieted as she kissed me lightly on the cheek. "You look cute! Maybe I need you in a tux every day," she teased.

"Yeah, whatever," I laughed, feeling the tension between us soften.

"Did my mom say hey to you?" she asked as we headed toward the door.

"She waved," I said, trying to downplay the awkwardness.

"Natalie, say hey to T.J.!" Natalie called back, but before her mom could respond, her father stepped in.

"Step outside with me, son," he said, his voice suddenly polite, almost too polite. I shot Natalie a look, confused, but followed him out onto the porch. The door shut behind me, and I heard muffled voices inside. I edged closer to an open window, straining to hear.

"I'm not sending prom pictures with her and some black kid to the family. I refuse!" Natalie's father's voice was sharp, cutting through the silence like a knife.

No response. No protest from Natalie. Nothing but stillness. My legs felt like they were moving on their own, carrying me away from the house, back toward the bus stop. Part of me wished Natalie would chase after me, tell me it wasn't true, that she didn't agree with him.

But no one came.

As the bus pulled up, I watched the little purple corsage box tumble away in the wind, left behind like everything else that night.

Chapter 10

HANG ON TO YOUR LOVE

WALKING DOWN THE BOULEVARD from the bus stop, I tried

to keep my head low, but it was hard to hide from the old heads

posted up on benches. "Man, don't come over here selling them bean

pies!" one of them shouted, sending a wave of laughter through the

group. I smiled awkwardly but kept my pace. As I walked, I couldn't

shake the funny feeling that someone might snap a picture of me in

this damn tuxedo and post it all over social media. Like, who walks

around in a tuxedo in one of the most dangerous cities in the state?

The thought of going viral for all the wrong reasons made my

stomach knot. The weight of the afternoon felt heavier with every

step.

By the time I was close to the house, the heat of the day caught up to

me. I could feel the bigen sliding across my forehead even though I

asked the barber to not apply that to my hairline. "I gotta have you looking right for your prom pictures!", said Malik, my barber. I felt disgusted at this point while walking as if I slid my forehead across a cast-iron pan. All the while, I kept glancing at my phone, waiting for a message from Natalie—something, anything that showed she cared, that maybe she regretted what her father had said. But my phone stayed silent, mocking me.

As I rounded the corner, I spotted Sade outside, lounging in her mom's car, music spilling out of the speakers. I tried to slip past her unnoticed, desperate to avoid the inevitable questions about my tuxedo. But of course, Sade saw me. She burst out laughing, loud enough for the whole neighborhood to hear.

"Why do you look like a Paul bearer from Jenkins Funeral Home?" she teased, barely able to get the words out through her laughter. Then, with a playful grin, she added, "Damn bro, you dressed like you on the third episode of *Married at First Sight*."

Normally, I would've thrown a joke right back, but today I couldn't. I was too tired, too embarrassed, too drained. Sade noticed the shift in my mood. Her laughter faded, and her face softened as she asked, "What's wrong?"

I told her everything—Natalie's father, the tuxedo, the long, humiliating walk home. She listened carefully, and when I was done, she stepped closer and asked if she could hug me. I nodded, and the hug she gave me was one of the best I'd ever had, even better than Aunt Nina's famous bear hugs. There was a comfort in it, a realness that hit me harder than I expected.

After we pulled apart, Sade confided in me. She was nervous about prom, feeling the weight of expectations, but not for the reasons I thought. She was scared of losing her virginity, scared that Jermaine, her boyfriend, would leave her if she didn't go through with it. The pressure from his teammates, the locker room talk, the stupid jokes—it all weighed on her. "I want to marry him," she said, her voice shaking a little, "like those high school sweethearts you see in movies. But I'm afraid I'm gonna mess it all up."

She paused for a moment, then her eyes lit up with an idea. "What if you came with me to prom? We could make Natalie jealous, post pictures of us together, and maybe... It'll take some pressure off me with Jermaine. It'll buy me some time, you know?"

I wasn't sure at first, but the more she talked, the more it made sense. And honestly, after the day I had, I could use a win, even if it was a petty one. So, I agreed.

As we sat there, Sade making plans, I felt my phone buzz. I glanced down and saw a flood of messages, all with links to Natalie's Instagram. She was posting pictures and videos from the dance, all smiles, having the time of her life. Dedric called next.

"I don't hear no music in the background or see you in any of her pictures. Where are you at, bro?" His voice was loud, cutting through whatever fragile peace I'd found in Sade's car.

I didn't have the energy to explain. Dedric was always blunt, always demanding answers I didn't have. I hung up, staring at the empty text thread from Natalie, and wondered how I ended up here—waiting for something that was never going to come.

The road back to the house felt long, but not as long as the journey I'd been on with Natalie. And in that moment, with Sade by my side, I realized something: hanging on to love wasn't supposed to feel like this.

Chapter 11

SESSION THREE

Therapy Session

TJ SAT IN DR. PHARR'S OFFICE, his foot tapping softly on the floor, a nervous energy buzzing in the silence between them. The familiar scent of sandalwood filled the room, a constant in these sessions, but today, something felt heavier. It had been weeks since TJ had visited Dr. Pharr, and the unspoken tension weighed down on his chest.

"So, TJ, you mentioned you wanted to talk about something from your past, something that's been on your mind a lot lately," Dr. Pharr began, her voice calm yet probing.

TJ looked up, meeting her gaze, then quickly looked away. The memories clawed at the edges of his mind, begging to be let out. "Yeah, I've been thinking about this... this thing from years ago. I haven't talked about it in years, but it's been sitting heavy with me recently."

Dr. Pharr waited, her hands resting lightly on the notepad in front of her, always patient, always letting TJ find his own pace.

"It was prom night," TJ finally said, his voice thick. "I was 15. It was supposed to be this magical night, you know? With Natalie. She was… everything. My first real love, I guess."

He paused, taking a deep breath. The images flashed through his mind: Natalie's bright smile, the way she twirled in her prom dress, how perfect everything seemed. Until it wasn't.

"But it wasn't magical, was it?" Dr. Pharr prompted softly.

TJ shook his head. "No. It wasn't."

He shifted in his chair, his voice dropping lower, like he was still trying to hide from the memory. "Her dad… he didn't want me there. Didn't want me with his daughter. I knew he didn't like me, but I never knew why until that night."

TJ's jaw clenched, and he stared hard at the floor. "He told her and her mom that Natalie wasn't going to prom with some Black boy.

Said it like it was a curse, like I was dirty. Like I wasn't even human."

Dr. Pharr remained silent, letting the words sink in. TJ could feel the heat rising in his chest, even after all these years. He wasn't done. Not yet.

"Then, I overheard him whispering to his wife." TJ continued, the pain lacing his words. "He said he wasn't sending out any prom pictures with a… with a 'nigger' in them. I'll never forget that word coming out of his mouth. It was like a punch to the gut."

The word lingered in the air, ugly and raw, like a wound that had never fully healed.

"It was the first time I ever really faced that kind of racism," TJ said, his voice trembling with the weight of it. "I grew up in the city, surrounded by people who looked like me. I didn't realize people still thought like that. That people could be that hateful."

Dr. Pharr nodded slowly. "How did you feel, standing there, hearing that?"

"Like I didn't belong. Like I wasn't good enough, no matter what I did." TJ's voice cracked, and for the first time in a long time, he felt the sting of tears. "I tried to brush it off. I smiled, went home, and pretended it didn't bother me. But deep down... deep down, I was shattered."

He looked up at Dr. Pharr, his eyes glassy. "I didn't realize it then, but I think that night changed me. It made me start thinking that no matter what, people were always going to see me as less. And if Natalie's dad didn't think I was good enough for his daughter, then... why would any woman? Why would anyone?"

Dr. Pharr leaned forward slightly. "Do you think that experience has shaped how you approach relationships now?"

TJ nodded, slowly at first, then with more certainty. "Yeah. Yeah, I think it has. I think it's why I can't trust women. Why do I care so damn much about what people think of me? I keep waiting for them to turn on me, you know? To look at me the way her father did. Like I'm nothing."

He paused, rubbing his hands together as if trying to scrub away the lingering shame. "I leave relationships before they can hurt me. Before I get blindsided again. Because if I leave first, I'm in control. I don't have to feel that pain. That rejection."

Dr. Pharr's voice was soft but firm. "But in doing that, you're cutting off your chance at real connection. You're letting the past dictate your present."

"I know," TJ whispered. "But it's hard to shake. That night... it wasn't just about racism. It was about being rejected on a deeper level. Like I wasn't worthy of love, of respect."

Dr. Pharr nodded again. "That's a heavy burden to carry, TJ. And it's not something you should have to bear alone. But if we don't confront it, it will keep driving you. Keep shaping your relationships."

TJ sat back, feeling the exhaustion in his bones. "I guess that's why I'm here, right? To figure this shit out."

Dr. Pharr smiled gently. "Exactly. And you've already taken the first step. You're recognizing where it began, how it's shaped you. Now we work on how to break free from it."

TJ stared at the ceiling, feeling the weight of years pressing down on him. But in the midst of that weight, there was a flicker of hope. Maybe, just maybe, he could start to let go of the pain that had followed him for so long.

As the session wound down, TJ wiped his eyes, letting the tears fall freely. He wasn't the 15-year-old boy from prom night anymore, but part of him still carried that pain. And maybe it was time to start setting it down.

"I'm ready," TJ whispered. "I don't know how yet... but I'm ready to stop running."

Chapter 12

FORBIDDEN FRUIT

TWO WEEKENDS BEFORE THE PROM, the pressure was on. Sade was excited about her dress, the flowers, the entire night—it was all she talked about. Meanwhile, I was sweating the money. It wasn't like my parents had it laying around. I had to figure something out fast.

That's when I called my uncle, who ran his own construction business. I asked if I could help out that weekend to earn some cash. He chuckled over the phone, telling me, "Ain't much work right now, kid. We're dealing with an apartment building, and trust me, it's too dangerous for you to be around." My heart sank, but he quickly added, "But... there's a simple job you and your cousin can handle. Some old man on the other side of town needs a wheelchair ramp built. You two can handle that, easily."

The thought of working near Natalie's house, even if by coincidence, gave me an extra push to say yes. I called my cousin, and the plan was set.

That Saturday morning, we rolled up to the house. It was quiet. Not a soul in sight except for this girl about my age, lounging on the porch in an oversized white tee. She didn't say much, just nodded as we pulled out our tools. My cousin shot her a glance but kept moving.

"Hey, are the owners here?" I asked, more out of formality than curiosity.

"Nope, but they said y'all could go ahead and start," she answered, her tone lazy and uninterested.

We got to work. Mixing mortar, laying down the foundation—it wasn't hard, just tedious. Still, something felt off. While we worked, we kept hearing these muffled grunts and odd sounds coming from inside the house. My cousin and I exchanged looks, but we didn't dare investigate. The last thing we needed was for this girl to run inside and call her grandparents, saying we were snooping.

Then, just as we were about to finish, I heard the back door creak open. From the reflection off my glasses, I saw someone stepping out. Nike slides, an orange football shirt—the jersey from our school's 7-on-7 team.

I turned slowly and locked eyes with Jermaine The star wide receiver. He froze for a second, clearly not expecting to see me there. His usual cocky smirk was replaced with a look of pure panic.

The girl in the oversized tee stepped down from the porch and went straight to Jermaine's car, throwing her arms around him and kissing him like they'd been a couple for years. She glanced back at me and my cousin. "Y'all know each other?" she asked, looking between Jermaine and me.

Jermaine scratched the back of his neck, trying to play it cool. "Yeah, he's... uh, the football team's manager."

I nodded, trying to suppress the confusion and awkwardness brewing inside me. The girl shrugged, uninterested in the details, and sauntered back into the house, leaving me and Jermaine standing there in tense silence.

Jermaine quickly stepped toward me, lowering his voice. "Yo, TJ, man... you gotta keep this between us. Don't tell Sade, aight?"

I stared at him for a moment, feeling a knot form in my stomach. I nodded, barely able to get the word "Yeah" out of my mouth.

He gave me a quick nod of thanks and rushed back to his car, peeling out of the driveway like he had somewhere more important to be.

I stood there, stunned, a thousand thoughts racing through my head. Sade, Jermaine, this girl. What the hell was I supposed to do? I couldn't get the image out of my mind—Jermaine's nervous face, the way he held his breath when she kissed him.

Later that night, I couldn't shake the unease. I called up a friend from Peninsula High. "Yo," I started, hesitant, "you know a girl named Izzy? Lives in Park Landing?"

His laugh came through the phone before he even answered. "Bro, that's the school thot. She's got as much DNA in her as Dexter's blood slides. She'll let a seventh grader hit if they ask the right way."

I sat there in silence, my phone heavy in my hand. Suddenly, the world around me seemed darker. Jermaine and Izzy. Jermaine and Sade.

I wasn't sure what to feel—betrayed, disgusted, or maybe... relieved that it wasn't my problem. But something about that moment, the secrets I was now forced to keep, felt like a turning point. Another weight on my shoulders, one I didn't ask for but couldn't shrug off.

At that moment, the world felt twisted—like the game was rigged, and I was just starting to figure out how deep it all went.

Chapter 13

SPARKS WILL FLY

PROM NIGHT WAS SUPPOSED TO BE MAGICAL, or at least that's what everyone told me. I was standing in Sade's living room, the smell of her mom's perfume lingering in the air as our mothers fussed over every little detail—our outfits, our hair, even the way we stood. Sade's green dress shimmered under the soft light, hugging her curves in a way that made her look older, more mature. I caught myself staring, feeling out of place in my suit, like I was pretending to be someone I wasn't.

"Smile!" Sade's mom chirped, snapping pictures with her phone. My mom stood beside her, equally giddy, their excitement almost infectious.

"What's your number?" Sade's mom asked as we were walking to the car. "I'll send you these pictures."

I handed her my phone, trying to ignore the knot forming in my stomach. Prom night jitters, I figured.

The drive to prom started out quiet. Too quiet. Sade stared out the window, her fingers tapping lightly against the armrest. I tried to think of something to say, but before I could, she spoke.

"TJ, I have to tell you something."

I glanced at her, my heart pounding a little faster. "Yeah?"

She hesitated, then sighed. "I lost my virginity to Jermaine yesterday."

It felt like the air had been sucked out of the car. My grip tightened on the seatbelt as I tried to process what she just said. Jermaine? Yesterday?

"I... What? Why?" I stammered, not sure what else to say.

Sade sighed again, leaning back in her seat. "I felt like I had to. He told me it was fine that I was going to prom with you because he had a football thing, but I don't know... I felt guilty."

I swallowed hard, the weight of her words pressing down on me. "You didn't have to do that. You didn't owe him anything."

"I know that now," she said, her voice small. "But it felt like... I don't know. Like it was something I needed to do to make things even."

Silence settled between us, heavy and uncomfortable. My mind raced, trying to make sense of it all. I felt guilty, too, like somehow this was my fault.

"How was it?" I blurted out, regretting the question immediately.

"It wasn't all that," she said, a bitter laugh escaping her lips. "It could've waited."

I didn't know what to say. Part of me wanted to comfort her, but the other part was still trying to untangle my own feelings. Before I could say anything, my phone buzzed. It was a text from Sade's mom with the pictures she had taken earlier. I opened it, and the message beneath the photos made me chuckle.

"It's time to turn into Petty Murphy on social media LOL. Make that little white girl jealous for me!"

I showed the text to Sade, and we both started laughing, the tension finally breaking. For a moment, it felt normal—like we were just two kids going to prom, no baggage, no complicated feelings.

At the after-prom party, I did exactly what Sade's mom suggested. I posted every picture—me and Sade smiling, posing, looking like we were having the time of our lives. It didn't take long for Natalie, my ex, to blow up my phone.

I didn't even bother reading most of the messages. I blocked her after the last one came through: *Black dudes are so sensitive. You'll definitely be the last one.*

I showed Sade the text, and she didn't even hesitate. She grabbed my arm, pulling me out of the bowling alley.

"We're going to the store," she said, determination written all over her face.

"For what?" I asked, still trying to catch up.

"Eggs and bologna."

I stared at her, confused. "Are you hungry or something? We could've just gone to Waffle House."

Sade rolled her eyes. "No, TJ. We're getting revenge."

A few minutes later, we were standing in the fluorescent glow of the convenience store, a carton of eggs and several packs of bologna in our hands. I still didn't fully understand what was happening, but I went along with it.

Sade tossed the items onto the counter and turned to me. "Put Natalie's address in the GPS."

It finally clicked. "Wait, you're serious?"

"Dead serious."

We pulled up to Natalie's house, and Sade was all business. She handed me two eggs. "Throw these once I'm back in the car."

I did as I was told, watching as she carefully placed slices of bologna all over Natalie's old, beat-up Honda Accord. The eggs splattered against the car, a satisfying crack echoing through the quiet neighborhood. When she was done, Sade got back in the car and told me to hold the steering wheel.

"What for?" I asked, a little nervous now.

Sade grinned, leaning out the back window with an egg in her hand. "Just drive."

I held the wheel steady as she launched egg after egg, her aim scarily accurate as they hit their mark. I couldn't help but laugh, the absurdity of the whole situation was sinking in. Here we were, on prom night, egging my ex's car and covering it with bologna. It was ridiculous, but it felt good.

By the time we left, the car was a mess—yolk dripping down the sides, slices of bologna sticking to the windows. It was petty, childish even, but in that moment, I didn't care.

The next morning, Natalie posted pictures of her ruined car, and all I could do was laugh. Her Honda looked like it had been through a food fight, and the comments were ruthless. She didn't know it was us, but that didn't matter.

As I stared at the photos, I realized something. Maybe Sade was right. Maybe being nice and responsible didn't get you far. Maybe sparks really did fly when you stopped caring what people thought.

And for the first time, I was okay with that.

Chapter 14

IT IS NEVER AS GOOD AS THE FIRST TIME

WE PULLED INTO THE DRIVEWAY, the glow from the streetlamp casting long shadows across the lawn. Sade sat beside me, quiet after coming from the movies, her fingers nervously fidgeting with the hem of her shirt. I thought maybe she was just lost in thought, but as we approached the house, I noticed something off.

Ms. Anderson was on the porch, her shoulders hunched as if the weight of the world had just fallen on her. Her face was buried in her hands, her entire body trembling with sobs. The porch light flickered above her, casting an eerie glow on the scene.

Sade froze. "Mom?"

Ms. Anderson looked up, her eyes bloodshot, tears streaming down her face. "She's gone, baby... Grandma's gone."

The words hung in the air like a thick fog, suffocating and heavy. Sade's hand shot to her mouth, a quiet gasp escaping her lips. Without thinking, she bolted out of the car, rushing to her mother's side. I sat there for a moment, trying to process what had just happened.

I followed her to the porch, unsure of what to say or do. Sade cradled her mother in her arms, whispering words of comfort that I couldn't hear. I stood there, helpless, unsure of what to do with myself. Sade's grandmother had passed away just five minutes ago. The reality of it hit like a sledgehammer. I had no idea what to say, how to make this better. So, I did the only thing I knew how to do—I stayed.

For the next two weeks, things were... different. The Sade I knew was gone, replaced by someone quieter, more distant. She spent her time with her mom, barely talking to anyone, not even me. But I didn't give up. Every day, I checked in. Whether it was a simple text or showing up at the door with food, I made sure they knew I was there.

Dedric, Bryson, and I even showed up one night with Hamburger Helper, a pathetic attempt at lifting their spirits, but it worked—at least a little. "You boys and that Hamburger Helper," Ms. Anderson laughed through her tears, thanking me for being so thoughtful. She kept saying I was like family now, and that meant more than she could know. I smiled, but inside I felt like I wasn't doing enough.

Sade texted me every night. Sometimes just to vent, sometimes just to say thanks. It wasn't much, but it was something. And that's all I could ask for.

Then one night, I was alone in my house. My mom was at work, the place eerily quiet except for the soft hum of the TV in the background. My phone buzzed. It was Sade.

Sade: Can I come over?

I didn't hesitate. Me: Door open.

Minutes later, she was standing in my living room, her eyes tired, her face worn from weeks of holding everything together. She didn't say much. Just collapsed onto the couch next to me, her body close but not touching mine. We sat there in silence for what felt like an eternity before she spoke.

"Jermaine hasn't really been there for me," she whispered, her voice barely audible. "I mean, he texts me, but... he hasn't come over, hasn't even called much."

I nodded, not sure what to say. I knew Jermaine was distant, but this felt... different. Wrong.

"But you've been here," she continued, turning to face me. "You've been here for me and my mom. And I just... I appreciate it, TJ."

I didn't know what to say. I opened my mouth to respond, but before I could, she moved closer, her hand brushing against mine. Then, she hugged me, pulling me into her warmth. It wasn't just a friendly hug—it was something more, something heavier.

When she pulled back, her face was inches from mine. Her eyes searched mine, and then, without warning, she kissed me. It was soft at first, hesitant, like she was testing the waters. My heart pounded in my chest, and before I knew it, I was kissing her back.

She pulled away just slightly, her breath warm against my lips. "Are you a virgin?" she asked, her voice low.

I swallowed hard, my throat suddenly dry. "Yeah... I am."

Sade paused, her eyes locked on mine. "Do you want to lose it?"

I didn't know how to answer, but the words slipped out before I could stop them. "That'd be cool."

She smiled softly, almost sadly, before pulling me in again, her lips capturing mine with more urgency this time. My heart raced, every nerve in my body on high alert as she guided me through something I had only ever imagined in fleeting daydreams. It wasn't like I thought it would be—there was no grand, cinematic moment, no fireworks exploding in the background. It was awkward at first, fumbling hands and nervous touches, but Sade was patient, and I tried my best to match her pace.

The room felt impossibly hot, the air thick with tension as we moved together, the rest of the world fading into the background. This wasn't how I'd imagined losing my virginity, but at that moment, it didn't matter. All that mattered was her, and the way she made me feel.

When it was over, we lay there in silence, both of us catching our breath. Sade rested her head on my chest, her fingers tracing circles on my skin. I didn't know what to say, so I said nothing, just held her close, trying to make sense of what had just happened.

Eventually, she got up, kissed me one last time, and left, her scent lingering in the air long after she was gone.

The next day at school, I couldn't shake the weight of what had happened. It wasn't regret, exactly—it was more complicated than that. But I knew one thing for sure: I couldn't just stand by and watch Jermaine keep screwing up.

I found him after lunch, pulling him aside by the lockers. "Look, man, you need to take better care of Sade. She's been through a lot, and she deserves someone who's actually there for her."

Jermaine stared at me for a long moment, his expression unreadable. "What're you talking about, TJ?"

I sighed, running a hand through my hair. "I'm talking about you not showing up for her. She needs you, and you're not there."

He didn't say anything at first, just looked at me like he was trying to figure out if I was serious. Finally, He scoffed, shaking his head. "Man, you don't know what you're talking about."

But I did know. I knew that while Jermaine was off somewhere else, Sade was leaning on me for support. And now, everything between us had changed in a way I wasn't sure I could ever undo.

It wasn't as good as I'd thought it would be—losing it, crossing that line. There was no magic moment, no fireworks. Just a quiet, complicated mess of emotions I didn't know how to deal with.

And for the first time, I wondered if this was how things started to fall apart.

Chapter 15

KING OF SORROW

TWO WEEKS PASSED, and Sade's texts became fewer, shorter, more distant. It was like she'd slowly slipped away into the fog of Jermaine's shadow. Each time my phone buzzed, I hoped it was her, only to be disappointed by a group chat or some pointless notification. It felt like being dropped from someone's life without warning, and it gnawed at me in ways I wasn't prepared for.

Spring break came, but instead of the freedom and fun it promised, all I could think about was Sade—and the last time we were together. Two weeks had passed since we had sex, and I was stuck in my head. It wasn't just the emotional stuff, either. Every night, like clockwork, I'd have these intense, vivid dreams. Wet dreams, one after the other, as if my body was taunting me with the memory of something I hadn't even fully processed.

Then one morning, I woke up, and the reality hit hard. There was something wrong. I pulled back the covers, groggy, and then panic set in—green discharge, right there around my genitals. I could hardly breathe. My mind raced, jumping to all the worst conclusions. I didn't dare Google it. I was convinced that one quick search would tell me I was dying. Genital cancer? Some rare disease? Whatever it was, it couldn't be good.

I wanted to talk to someone—anyone—but how do you start that conversation? "Hey, mom, there's green stuff coming out of me." Yeah, right.

So instead, I took the long way around. "Hey, mom, could you grab me a pamphlet from work? For a school project?" My mom worked in the medical field, so it wasn't completely out of the blue. "Something on STDs," I added, trying to sound casual, like it was no big deal.

She barely blinked. "Sure thing, I'll bring one home tomorrow."

But the next day came, and the burning started. I felt it every time I used the bathroom, and my mind spiraled into the worst places. What if this was it? What if I was seriously messed up now? To make matters worse, my testicles started to feel swollen, aching in a way that wasn't normal. I couldn't just sit there and wait for the pamphlet like some kind of slow death sentence.

I ended up at the clinic, hoping they could tell me it was nothing. But when they mentioned using a Q-tip to test for STDs, I froze. A Q-tip? In my urethra? The thought alone was enough to make me break out in a cold sweat. I bailed, convincing myself I could wait it out. Maybe this would all just... go away.

It didn't.

The symptoms kept getting worse. I found myself back at the clinic days later, this time too freaked out to back down. Thankfully, they used a urine test, no Q-tips involved. The nurse assured me the results would take about a week, but that week felt like a lifetime. Every time my phone rang or I got an email, I braced for the news.

Finally, the call came. My heart pounded in my chest as I answered, my mouth dry.

"Is this TJ?"

"Yeah, it's me."

"Your results came back positive for chlamydia."

The world around me blurred for a moment. Chlamydia. I'd heard about it in health class, sure, but it felt different when it was real— when it was happening to me. The nurse's voice was calm, professional. She explained that it was treatable, that I'd be okay if I followed the medication instructions.

But none of that stuck. All I heard was the confirmation of my worst fear: I had an STD. Me. The guy who had only been with one girl. The guy who was supposed to have control over his life, who thought he was smart and responsible.

For days after that, I couldn't shake the feeling of shame. I avoided everyone, even my own thoughts. I didn't want to think about how I ended up here, about the choices that led me to this point. But I couldn't escape it, no matter how hard I tried.

The reality settled in deep. The king of sorrow—that's what I felt like. Someone trapped in a mess of his own making, with no clear way out. And worse, I knew this was just the beginning.

Chapter 16

SESSION FOUR

Therapy Session

THE CLOCK ON THE WALL ticked steadily, filling the silence between me and Dr. Pharr. It had been days since I'd sat in this chair, yet the feeling was the same—an uncomfortable mix of dread and relief. Therapy had always been like that for me, pulling me in two directions at once. I wanted to talk, but I also wanted to keep my mouth shut.

Dr. Pharr leaned forward slightly, her notepad resting in her lap. "It's been a while, TJ. How are you feeling about being back?"

I shrugged, staring at the abstract painting on the wall behind her, trying to make sense of the swirls of color that didn't seem to go anywhere. "I don't know. Guess I feel the same way I did the last time I was here."

"And how was that?"

I let out a small laugh. "Like I'm dragging my feet through the mud, but still moving forward. Barely."

Dr. Pharr nodded, jotting something down. Her calmness had always annoyed me. She made everything seem like it had an easy answer, but we both knew it never was.

"So," she said, breaking the silence. "Let's talk about what's really on your mind. You mentioned you've been thinking about Sade lately, and the aftermath of what happened back in high school."

I sighed, shifting in my seat. I knew this was coming, but it didn't make it any easier. "Yeah. It's been messing with me more than usual."

"What part of it?"

"All of it," I replied, the weight of the memories pressing against my chest. "Losing my virginity to her, the chlamydia, everything that came after... it's like a scar that never really healed, you know? I thought I was over it, but it still lingers."

Dr. Pharr didn't rush me. She never did. I guess that's why I kept coming back to her, even when I wanted to avoid everything about this part of my past.

"It's weird," I continued. "I always thought that losing my virginity would be this big moment. Like, something that would make me feel different. And it did... but not in the way I expected."

Dr. Pharr waited, her pen poised over his notepad. "How did it make you feel, TJ?"

"Broken," I said, the word hanging in the air between us. "It didn't feel special. It felt like... a mistake. And then, when I found out about the chlamydia, it was like the universe was punishing me for even trying to be close to someone."

"Do you think that experience shaped how you see relationships now?"

I laughed again, this time bitterly. "Shaped? It shattered everything. After that, I stopped trusting people. I stopped letting women in. Every relationship I've had since then, it's like I'm waiting for the other shoe to drop. Like I'm going to get hurt or screwed over, so I leave before it can happen."

"And Sade? What role does she play in that?"

I hesitated, running a hand through my hair. Sade had been a constant ghost in my life, haunting my thoughts more than I wanted to admit. "She was my friend. My crush. And after everything... I couldn't even look at her the same. It wasn't her fault, but I blamed her anyway. I think I blamed her because it was easier than facing my own issues."

Dr. Pharr scribbled something on her pad before looking up at me. "You mentioned your children before, in previous sessions. How do you think your experience with Sade, and the aftermath of losing your virginity, has impacted the way you've fathered them?"

I swallowed hard, feeling that familiar knot in my stomach. The truth was something I wasn't proud of, but it was part of why I was here.

"I wasn't ready to be a father. I mean, I know no one is ever really ready, but for me... it's like I became this person who saw women as either something to avoid or something to use. I didn't think about the consequences, about the kids who'd come into the world because of my mistakes."

Dr. Pharr leaned in, her voice gentle but firm. "So when you call them 'bastards,' you're not just talking about the circumstances of their birth. You're talking about the way you see yourself as their father."

I nodded, the weight of that realization sinking in. "Yeah. I mean, I've always been there financially. I've done what's expected. But emotionally? I've kept them at arm's length. It's like... I don't want them to get too close, because what if I screw them up, too?"

Dr. Pharr was quiet for a moment, letting the air clear between us. "TJ, you're here because you're trying to understand why you became the person you are today. But it's important to realize that you can change. You can choose to be a different man, a different father."

I knew she was right, but it didn't feel that simple. "How do I do that, though? How do I stop feeling like this?"

"It starts with forgiveness," she said, her voice steady. "Forgiveness for Sade. Forgiveness for yourself. You've been carrying this weight for too long, TJ. It's time to put it down."

The room fell silent again, the clock ticking away the seconds. I stared down at my hands, wondering if I was capable of letting go. Could I really forgive myself for all the damage I'd caused? For the relationships I'd ruined, for the children I'd kept at a distance, for the man I'd become?

"I don't know if I can," I whispered.

Dr. Pharr's eyes met mine, filled with the same calm patience they always held. "You can. But it's going to take time. And it's going to take honesty—honesty with yourself, and with the people you care about."

I nodded, even though I wasn't sure I believed her. But I was here. I was trying. And maybe, just maybe, that was enough for now.

As the session ended, I stood up to leave, the weight still heavy on my shoulders but feeling a little lighter than before. It wasn't much, but it was something. A step forward, however small.

Maybe, this time, I wouldn't drag my feet through the mud.

Chapter 17

WINDOW PAIN

I STARED AT MY PHONE, the screen glowing in the dark, mocking me with the unread message from the clinic. My mind raced, stomach churning with a cocktail of dread and guilt. Telling Sade felt like signing my own death warrant, but keeping it from her felt worse—like dragging both of us deeper into a fire I had already lit.

I had to talk to someone, and Bryson and Dedric were always the first in line. I figured they'd help me clear my head and give me some advice. Instead, they made things more complicated—but in a way only real friends could.

"Yo, y'all busy?" I texted in the group chat.

Within minutes, they showed up. Bryson swung open the door to my room, his usual grin already plastered on his face.

"What's up, man?" Dedric followed close behind, a bag of chips in hand. "Why the serious face?"

I didn't even know how to start. I sat on the edge of my bed, shaking my head, the words caught in my throat.

"Y'all, it's bad," I finally managed to get out. "I've got...chlamydia."

The room fell silent for a second, like the air had been sucked out. Bryson blinked, his grin fading into pure confusion. Dedric froze, mid-chew, staring at me like I'd just told them I was dying.

Then, the explosion came.

"Wait, wait, wait!" Bryson practically screamed. "You had sex? When did this happen?"

I nodded, my face hot with embarrassment. "Yeah, man. With Sade."

Dedric coughed, chips flying everywhere. "Hold up, hold up! You finally got it in and now you're burning? Bruh!"

And then the laughter started. They laughed so hard I thought they were going to choke. Bryson grabbed his phone and immediately pulled up Nelly's "Hot in Herre," blasting the chorus as he doubled over, gasping for breath. Dedric followed suit, shouting out random lyrics from Lil Wayne's "Fire Man" and laughing until his eyes watered.

"Y'all ain't shit," I muttered, crossing my arms. But honestly, if the roles were reversed, I'd be doing the same thing. It was just our way. The way we held each other down was through laughter—sometimes at each other's expense. That's just how it was

It wasn't until Bryson pulled up Usher's "Let it Burn" that I finally cracked a smile, shaking my head. I let them have their fun, knowing it would die down eventually. And it did.

After a few more jokes, the laughter slowed, and reality crept back in. Bryson sat down next to me, still wiping tears from his eyes.

"Aight, man. For real," he said, his tone finally serious. "You gotta tell her."

"I know," I sighed. "But how?"

Dedric sat on the floor, leaning back against my bed. "Hell yeah, dawg. No games. Just tell her. She deserves to know."

Bryson nodded in agreement. "Better to hear it from you than to end up like one of those 'I found out through a friend' situations. Trust me."

As much as I dreaded the idea, they were right. I knew they were right.

So, I grabbed my phone and shot Sade a text: *Come over tonight after my mom goes to work. We need to talk.*

Her response was quick. *What's up?*
Just come over, I replied.

I couldn't sit still after that. My nerves were shot. I paced back and forth in my room, going over the conversation in my head a thousand times. What was I even supposed to say? There's no easy way to drop something like that on someone. Especially not someone like Sade.

She showed up just after 8, wearing one of her usual oversized hoodies and some sweats. Comfortable. She had no idea what was coming.

"Hey, what's up?" she asked, her eyes scanning my face for clues. She could already tell something was off.

I swallowed hard and sat down on the edge of my bed, motioning for her to sit beside me. She hesitated but joined me.

"I gotta tell you something. It's serious," I started, my voice already shaking.

"What's going on, TJ?" Her tone shifted, concerned replacing the usual carefree attitude.

"I, uh…" I struggled to get the words out, but I knew there was no turning back now. "I went to the clinic. I, uh, I got tested. And…I have chlamydia."

At first, she blinked, processing the information, her mouth slightly open like she didn't hear me right. Then she laughed, like it was a joke.

"Boy, stop playing. This better not be one of your dumbass pranks."

I shook my head. "I'm serious, Sade."

Her expression changed instantly, laughter dying in her throat. "What the hell, TJ? Are you for real?"

I nodded. "Yeah. I got it."

Her face twisted with anger, tears welling up in her eyes. "I knew it! You probably got it from that nasty-ass Natalie, didn't you? You've been messing around with her, haven't you?"

"No, no!" I stood up, running my hands through my hair, frustrated. "Sade, you took my virginity! You're the only person I've been with!"

She stood up, her body trembling with rage. "So you're saying I gave you chlamydia? Me?!"

"I'm just saying...you're the only person I've been with. It has to be—"

"Shut the hell up, TJ!" she shouted, storming toward the door. "You really gonna sit here and blame me for this? You're a sick, nasty piece of shit. Don't ever call me again!"

Before I could say anything else, she slammed the door and left, her footsteps echoing down the hallway. I stood there, frozen, my heart pounding in my chest. She was gone.

I collapsed onto the bed, burying my face in my hands. The pain hit me in waves, but not just physical. It was the kind of pain that settled deep inside—the kind that leaves a scar.

She blocked me on everything. No texts. No calls. No nothing.

And just like that, I was alone again.

Chapter 18

FOR YOUR EYES ONLY

I HADN'T SPOKEN to Sade in days, and the silence was killing me. Every time I checked my phone, a part of me hoped there'd be a message, something—anything. But there was nothing, just the empty void of her absence. She had cut me off, and all because she thought I gave her chlamydia.

Jermaine's results came back negative, and Sade immediately pointed the finger at me. It didn't matter how much I tried to explain myself, to tell her that it wasn't me. She didn't want to hear it. And now, I was left sitting in my room, alone, trying to piece together what had gone so horribly wrong.

That morning, my mom came into my room with that look on her face—serious, but trying to soften the blow with some sort of motherly care. "TJ," she said, crossing her arms like she was about to give me a lecture. "I need to talk to you. You gotta be careful out here. There's been a lot of kids in the ER for STDs like chlamydia."

I froze. How did she know? Was I that obvious?

"You better watch for these little fast-ass girls out here, TJ," she said, as if that was the real problem. In my head, I wanted to yell at her, to defend Sade, to tell her that Sade wasn't like that. Sade wasn't "fast." But what would be the point? She wouldn't understand. Moms never do.

Then she paused and said something that nearly knocked me out of my chair. "I know I'm breaking all kinds of HIPAA violations telling you this, but there's this boy from your football team who came in a couple weeks ago and tested positive for it. His name's Jermaine, I think. You better not tell anyone I said that, boy!"

I didn't need to say anything; the look of shock on my face said it all. Jermaine? The same Jermaine who had been lying to Sade and making her think I was the one?

I should've been relieved, but all I felt was anger. Anger at Jermaine for lying, anger at Sade for believing him, and anger at myself for not speaking up sooner. He'd been treated two weeks ago. Two weeks, and no one said a word. The only reason I knew was because of my mom's job. And then, to make matters worse, I heard about Izzy, that girl everyone had been whispering about at school. She had exposed Jermaine for giving her chlamydia too. The rumors were all over Peninsula High by now.

The next day, I ran into Sade at the vending machine, of all places. She didn't look at me, didn't even acknowledge that I was standing just a few feet away. I watched her punch in the numbers for her drink, waiting for the right moment to say something. I had to tell her.

"Sade," I said, my voice low as I slipped her a note.

She stared at the paper for a second before shoving it into her pocket. I didn't know if she'd even read it, but I had to try. In the note, I pleaded with her to dig deep with Jermaine, to ask him the real questions. To find out the truth. It wasn't me.

I went home that night, frustrated and exhausted, burying myself in video games just to keep my mind off everything. But as I was playing, I heard a knock on the door. I paused the game, the sound of the knock echoing in my mind as I made my way over to open it.

When I did, there she was—Sade, standing there, tapping the small orange pill bottle against her hand. She didn't say much at first, just stood there, looking down at her feet. Then, in the softest voice I'd ever heard her use, she said, "You were right."

I blinked, trying to process what she was saying.

"I'm sorry," she continued, lifting the bottle slightly. "I shouldn't have blamed you."

And just like that, she turned and walked away, leaving me standing there with more questions than answers. She was gone before I could even respond, the sound of her footsteps fading down the hallway.

Weeks passed, and I didn't see much of Sade after that. We had cleared the air, but things were never the same between us. Then one day, I came home from school and noticed a moving truck in front of Sade's house. My heart sank. I ran inside, looking for answers.

"Mom, what's going on at Sade's house?" I asked, barely able to keep the panic out of my voice.

"They're moving," she said nonchalantly, like it was no big deal. "Her mom's taking her to live in her grandma's house now that she's passed."

I didn't know what to say. Sade was leaving, and I hadn't even had a real chance to make things right. The next few days blurred together as I watched the house next door slowly empty out. The moving truck eventually disappeared, and with it, any hope I had of fixing things with Sade.

She was gone, and so was any chance of undoing the mess that Jermaine had made. All I had left were the memories—of us, of what could've been, and of the person I was slowly becoming.

The bastard had finally formed.

Chapter 19

SESSION FIVE - THE MOON AND THE SKY

Therapy Session

TJ SLUMPED BACK IN THE LEATHER CHAIR, the familiar creak under his weight a quiet reminder that he had been in this exact spot too many times to count. Session five. Dr Pharr sat across from him, her eyes calm, probing but never pushing. He never thought he would be the type to sit in therapy—hell, no man in his family had ever dared to talk about their problems, much less sit with a stranger and open up. Yet, here he was.

"Let's pick up where we left off last time, TJ," Dr. Pharr began, her voice as steady as ever. "We were talking about how things began to shift for you—how you started becoming the man you are now."

TJ sighed, running his hand over his face. He was tired, but this was the good kind of tired, the one that made you feel like you were finally doing something right. "It's hard, you know? Realizing that I became this... bastard. Treating women like they were always going to hurt me. It's like, I expected them to be Sade."

At the mention of her name, a flicker of something passed in his chest, but he pushed it down. "She was the first one to really hurt me. And I carried that with me—hell, I built a wall with that pain. Every woman after her had to climb it, and most didn't even try. Can't blame them."

Dr. Pharr nodded, her pen poised over her notepad but not moving. She was listening, really listening, the way no one else ever had. "And Sade... she was your first love?"

TJ swallowed. "Yeah, she was. Thought she'd be the last, too. But that's not how it played out."

There was a silence in the room, not uncomfortable, just heavy with everything left unsaid. Dr. Pharr leaned in slightly, her gaze unwavering. "Do you think that's when you started to lose trust in women? After what happened with Sade?"

TJ chuckled, but there was no humor in it. "Yeah, I think so. I couldn't trust women after her. Not fully. I mean, how could I? She showed me that people can just leave, can just switch up on you like that. One minute, they're all in, and the next… they're gone. And it hurt."

He rubbed his hands together, the friction soothing in an odd way. "And because of that, I became what I feared. I started treating women like they didn't matter, like they were temporary, 'cause I was scared of getting hurt again. I let my past with her turn me into something ugly. I hurt them before they could hurt me."

Dr. Pharr sat back in her chair, crossing one leg over the other. "That's a significant realization, TJ. It's not easy to admit when you've been part of the problem."

He nodded slowly. "Yeah… I'm just glad my girl—my current girlfriend—talked me into coming here. She's the reason I even gave this therapy thing a shot. And I'm grateful for that."

Dr. Pharr tilted her head slightly. "You haven't mentioned her name yet. Is that intentional?"

TJ smirked, but kept his lips sealed. "Maybe," he said cryptically. "She came into my life out of nowhere. It was like 3 a.m., at this gas station of all places. We'd both just left the adult clubs on the other side of town, and we were both trying to grab some food. It was random, man. But it felt right, you know? Like it was supposed to happen."

Dr. Pharr gave him a small smile, clearly intrigued by this mystery woman. "And how has this relationship been different from your past ones?"

TJ took a deep breath. "She's different. She's helping me get closer to God, helping me be a better father, helping me love myself, which I never really did before. That's why I finally agreed to therapy. I can't keep running from myself. She's shown me that."

There was a warmth in his voice as he spoke, something new that hadn't been there in the first few sessions. "It's crazy, 'cause I've never felt accepted by someone's family like I do now. Her friends, her mom—they all like me. I never thought that mattered, but it does. It feels good."

Dr. Pharr glanced at the clock on her desk. "Our time is up for today, TJ," she said softly. "But I'm curious—do you want to continue therapy?"

TJ stood up, sliding his coat over his broad shoulders. He paused for a moment, then turned back to her with a grin. "Yeah. I think I'd like to keep going."

Dr. Pharr smiled as she gathered her notes, but just as TJ was about to leave, she asked, "You still haven't told me—what's her name?"

TJ stopped at the door, his hand on the knob. He turned back slowly, meeting Dr. Pharr's gaze. For a moment, the room felt heavy with all the unspoken things between him and his past.

He smiled, took a deep breath, and said, "Sade. Anderson."

With that, he walked out, leaving the weight of his confession hanging in the air like the moon that followed him home, a reminder that the past could linger, but the future was still unwritten.

As TJ stepped out into the cool evening air, he felt lighter. For the first time in a long time, he didn't feel like the bastard he had once been. Maybe therapy wasn't so bad after all.

"For so long, I believed my life was shaped by everyone else—their betrayals, their lies, their love twisted into weapons. I made it easy to blame them, to justify my anger, my indifference, my destruction. But sitting here now, with nowhere left to run from my own reflection, I see the truth: I became the thing I hated most. A coward hiding behind pain, a man who let his brokenness become a curse. And worse, I passed that curse down to innocent lives, turning my own children into bastards—just like me. I can't take back what I've done. I can't erase the wreckage. But maybe, just maybe, I can find a way to stop this poison from spreading further. If not for me, then for them. Because God knows, they deserve better than the man I was."

ABOUT THE AUTHOR

Ryan J. Norman is a former special educator and case manager with extensive experience at the alternative school level. He holds a Bachelor of Arts in Psychology from Norfolk State University, where his academic journey was shaped by his deep interest in understanding human behavior—a theme central to his writing.

Growing up in Portsmouth, Virginia, Ryan faced the harsh realities of inner-city life. From witnessing violence to experiencing homelessness as a child, he watched his mother prevail to provide stability in a turbulent environment. These formative experiences deeply influenced his worldview and ignited his passion for storytelling, which he discovered during his 12th-grade year while applying to colleges and his father helping him discover his talent.

Now an entrepreneur, youth advocate, and mentor, Ryan dedicates his life to helping young people in his community reach their full potential. His writing reflects the complexities of growth, identity, and redemption, drawing from both his personal struggles and professional experiences working with at-risk youth.